THE GO-BETWEEN

AMY HEST

ILLUSTRATED BY DyAnne DiSalvo-Ryan

Four Winds Press   New York

Maxwell Macmillan Canada   Toronto

Maxwell Macmillan International

New York   Oxford   Singapore   Sydney

For Grandma Rose, with love—A.H.

To my father, the biggest Giant fan
of all time, with love—D.D.-R.

Four Winds Press
Macmillan Publishing Company
866 Third Avenue
New York, NY 10022

Maxwell Macmillan Canada, Inc.
1200 Eglinton Avenue East
Suite 200
Don Mills, Ontario M3C 3N1

Macmillan Publishing Company is part of the
Maxwell Communication Group of Companies.
First American edition
Printed and bound in Hong Kong.

10 9 8 7 6 5 4 3 2 1

The text of this book is set in 13 point Cheltenham Light.
The art is a diazo print done with watercolors and
colored pencils and reproduced in full color.
Book design by Christy Hale

Library of Congress Cataloging-in-Publication Data
Hest, Amy.
The go-between / Amy Hest ; illustrated by DyAnne DiSalvo-Ryan.
p.   cm.
Summary: Lexi gets more than she bargained for when she acts as a
go-between for her grandmother and Mr. Singer.
ISBN 0-02-743632-2
[1. Grandmothers—Fiction.   2. Friendship—Fiction.   3. Love—
Fiction.]   I. DiSalvo-Ryan, DyAnne, ill.   II. Title.
PZ7.H4375Go   1992
[E]—dc20   90-24561

Right outside my building there's a newsstand. It's a small news-stand, painted green on the outside and green on the inside, with a stripe of red around the middle.

Mr. Murray Singer has worked that place for as long as anyone in this old neighborhood can remember…and that is pretty long! He is out there every single day…no matter what the weather is that day.

I know because my window faces Broadway, the big street.

One thing I love is getting up early and I am talking *very* early, such as six o'clock or even five-thirty. I listen for Gram's soft breathing in the bed across the room. She is always rolled into a ball, low down in her periwinkle quilt.

No matter what time it is, and sometimes it is still pitch black, I am never the first one up in *this* neighborhood.

Over at the all-night grocery, for example, it is business as usual. Those fellows never sleep, I think! They squat in rows on red milk crates. Slicing. Chopping. Making colorful pyramids on open stalls. Apples and oranges and snow pea pods. And things I never heard of. Soon the sun will slide over Central Park. Customers will line up then, for coffee and buns, tea and cheese Danish. And those tulips! They are red and pink and white, and sometimes, a sad shade of lavender. My favorites are the yellows, though.

City buses cough and sputter. Trucks and taxis, too. Early walkers trickle up from the side streets. A lot of them stop at the newsstand. They chat with Murray and he chats back, counting out change. Sometimes he tips his cap, but just to the ladies!

"Up so early?" Gram always says up-so-early and she comes, slowly, to the window. Wrapping her bathrobe on the way.

"Hello, it's raining." I always say hello-it's-this or hello-it's-that, and I kiss her satin cheek.

My grandmother loves early morning like I do, and she loves a rainy day. She puts her face to the wide window and right away she's smiling...at the morning and the rain, and at Murray Singer's banner.

FIRST GAME OF SEASON TUESDAY 7:30 GO-O-O YANKEES!

Everyone around here knows Murray Singer is some kind of baseball fan. (My grandmother is, too.) They say he knows every little thing about every little thing that has to do with that game. (So does she.) When it comes to rooting, though, he only roots for the New York teams. (Just like her.) And all through baseball season, he hangs signs that say things like METS GO FOR IT! or YANKEES #1 IN THE BRONX!

"Would you look at that old man…*soaked*!" Gram clucks. On cold, wet days like this one, Gram always sends down tea. She fixes it strong and steamy, in her best teapot with roses. Sometimes she adds a warm biscuit, too.

Murray sends back the morning paper. He likes to scratch a little message in the top right corner. His messages are fun. They say things like "Windy watch out!" or "Nice day for ducks!"

I run from my house to the newsstand and back again, and I am fast. They call me the go-between.

"Hello, Lexi!" Murray has the nicest sort of smile, and his collar is drawn against the wind.

"Teatime." I pour it from the porcelain pot. "Soaked?" I ask.

"Damp, not soaked." He sips the steaming tea and his glasses go foggy, but just for a minute, and we laugh. "How is your grandmother, anyway?"

"Good," I say. "Gram loves rainy days like this one."

Murray nods like he already knows that.

Customers come and go, and they are all in a hurry. Sometimes Murray lets me count out the change.

"Nice sign."

"Baseball," he says, "my second love."

"Second?" I say. "Then what is first?"

"A lady, Lexi, and I should have married *her* a long time ago."

"How come you didn't?" I catch a raindrop on my nose.

"How come, how come…" Murray hands me the morning paper.

Later, while my parents dress for work, Gram and I finish up the breakfast dishes. She washes. I dry. Then she walks me to school. Every single day. We pass the newsstand on the way.

"Morning, Mrs. G!" Murray tips his cap. "Lovely tea and I thank you!"

"Well *somebody* has to look out for you, since you don't look out for yourself." Gram pretends to bawl him out. "Stay out of the rain, Murray Singer, you're not a kid anymore!"

"And look who talks!" He always teases back but she likes it, I think.

Gram angles the purple umbrella. It is so big we take up most of the sidewalk, and people have to dance around us to get by.

"Who looks out for Murray," I wonder, "when he goes home at night?"

"He lives alone, Lexi."

"All alone? Not even a cat?"

"Not even a cat."

"That's sad," I say. "All alone, no one to come home to."

Gram doesn't answer. She must be thinking about my grampa, who died a long time ago, and I am glad she has me to come home to.

The light blinks DON'T WALK. A long car splashes muddy water at my knees, and I hop behind her fast.

"Tell me a secret, Gram, one about you when you were a girl on Grand Street."

"I think I've told them all." (She always says that.)

"Then tell me a story. Tell the one about you and Murray Singer and baseball."

"That one *again*?" (She always says that, too, and then she tells it.) "Murray and I have been friends for as long as I can remember…and that is pretty long. We lived on the same block when we were children, way downtown on Grand Street. There were trees, lots of them, and lovely rows of houses called brownstones.

"Now, Murray Singer," Gram goes on, "he was top-notch in the baseball department. Me? A one-girl fan club, perched on the stoop of number forty-five. I wasn't quiet about it, either!" she remembers. "I wrote chalk messages. I cheered and booed. I bossed until my voice went hoarse."

"Didn't you want to play?" I ask.

"And how. But *they* had a no-girl rule."

"That's dumb," I say.

"Double-dumb." Gram spins the big umbrella. "But once in a while those wiseacre boys were in a jam. Then they sent someone—and it was mostly Murray Singer—to see if I'd help out."

"And you did, of course."

"You bet. I showed *them* who was the number-on pitcher on Grand Street. Especially that Murray Singer!"

"Why *especially* Murray?"

"Well"—she lowers her voice—"to tell you the truth, I had the crush-of-the-world on Murray Singer!"

Now there's a secret I never heard before.

"A crush!" I cry. "Did you tell him?"

"Not on your life!"

"That's crazy, Gram. Some things shouldn't be secret."

The schoolyard is a wave of colorful slickers and umbrellas by the dozen. Gram walks me up the steps of the redbrick building. She always does.

"What if Murray had a crush on you, too?" I say. "What if he loves you still!"

"Ach, Lexi!" Gram waves her hand. "Murray and I are friends, really good friends, just like always. Besides," she adds, "I'm an old lady, set in her ways."

I kiss her cheek. "And who says you can't love an old lady?"

Next morning, and it's drizzly. Gram sends me down with tea.

Murray sips and says, "How is your grandmother, anyway?"

"Good," I answer. "She loves to talk about the old days on Grand Street."

"I can see her now—funny girl, boss of the world." Murray shakes his head, remembering. "Wow, could she pitch!"

"Gram says *you* were top-notch in the baseball department."

"She said that about me?" Murray looks pleased. "Lexi," he says, "can you keep a secret?"

"Sometimes."

"Your grandmother, she was cuter than anything. I was crazy about her!"

"Did you tell her?" I say.

"No way!"

"A person ought to tell a person that sort of thing."

"Yes, but sometimes it's hard to say."

"A person could even write it." I smile at Murray. "For example, in a message."

Murray rubs his chin. He wipes his glasses with a handkerchief. Then he finds a pencil, next to the box that holds his quarters. And he writes.

I run home fast to get ready for school. The morning paper is rolled with a rubberband, to keep the edges from curling. In the top right corner is a message from Murray. "Yankees tonight. Will Grand Street's #1 pitcher join me, please?"

I finish tying up my sneakers while Gram washes breakfast dishes. She is humming, I think, or maybe it's the radio.

"Are you going to Yankee Stadium?"

"You bet I am."

"But it's raining," I say.

"Can't rain forever, Lexi."

"But when will you be home?"

"I'll kiss you the minute I'm back," she says. "Fluff your pillows, too."

"Well, kiss me hard, and wake me. I want to know the score."

Morning, and a truck pulls up to the newsstand. There's always that man who drives and the other one, in back. He swings his arms left…right…left. Papers fly to the sidewalk. Murray gives a wave, then starts making tall, neat stacks. Stacks and stacks of morning news.

"Yankees won. Five-zip." Gram sings instead of talks, and she comes, not so slowly, to the window. "That Murray Singer is some nice fellow."

"Did you have a hot dog?" I ask.

"A scrumptious hot dog, and I shared a second one with Murray."

"Cracker Jacks, too?"

"Cracker Jacks, the works."

"I wish I could have been there."

"Murray says next time you come, too."

"He said that?"

Gram smiles. "I told you, Lexi, he's some nice fellow. I like him!"

"How much?" I ask. "How much do you like him?"

"Very much." Gram sketches squiggles on the misty window. "Funny, you know someone forever…and suddenly you're closer."

"You sound the way people sound in the movies." I trace a big heart on the window. "Are you in love?" I ask.

"Maybe a little." Gram giggles. "Imagine that!"

"But you and Murray are friends, just like always. And anyway, you are set in your ways…and what about me? And our room and our walks and talks and waking up early?"

"I love you, my Lexi. To pieces," Gram adds. "Some things may change, but nothing changes that."

"But what about Murray?"

"I can love you both. I can do that, Lexi." Gram gives me a hug. Then she gives me a message to run downstairs. "Great game, yummy hot dogs, I am crazy about Murray Singer."

"Hello!" he calls from the newsstand. "Hello, Miss Go-Between!"

"I think you'll like this message."

"Says who?"

"Says me."

Murray reads it fast, and he likes it all right. I know because his eyes are lightest gray and dancing.

Two months and two weeks into baseball season, my grandmother and Murray Singer get married! All day long, white streamers billow at the newsstand and there's a party, right there on Broadway. The best wedding party ever, and I wear a white dress. I carry tulips from the all-night grocer. My favorites, too, the yellows.

Now they work together at the newsstand in the morning and I watch them from my window. There's always that teapot with roses. Sometimes, well, actually more than sometimes, I wish Gram were here in our room, rolled up all cozy in her periwinkle quilt. My mother says don't be too set in your ways, Lexi, because things have a way of changing.

But some things *don't*, I say.

I stop by the newsstand on my way to school. Then Gram walks me over. Every single day…no matter what the weather is that day.